LIONEL
AT SCHOOL

LIONEL AT SCHOOL

by Stephen Krensky
pictures by Susanna Natti

PUFFIN BOOKS

For Brian
S.K.

To good friends Harry and Judith and Claire
S.N.

PUFFIN BOOKS
Published by the Penguin Group
Penguin Putnam Books for Young Readers, 345 Hudson Street, New York, New York 10014, U.S.A.
Penguin Books Ltd, 80 Strand, London WC2R ORL, England
Penguin Books Australia Ltd, Ringwood, Victoria, Australia
Penguin Books Canada Ltd, 10 Alcorn Avenue, Toronto, Ontario, Canada M4V 3B2
Penguin Books (N.Z.) Ltd, 182-190 Wairau Road, Auckland 10, New Zealand

Penguin Books Ltd, Registered Offices: Harmondsworth, Middlesex, England

First published in the United States of America by Dial Books for Young Readers,
a division of Penguin Putnam Books for Young Readers, 2000
Published by Puffin Books, a division of Penguin Putnam Books for Young Readers, 2002

1 3 5 7 9 10 8 6 4 2

THE LIBRARY OF CONGRESS HAS CATALOGED THE DIAL EDITION AS FOLLOWS:
Krensky, Stephen.
Lionel at school/by Stephen Krensky; pictures by Susanna Natti.—1st ed.
p. cm.—(Dial easy-to-read)
Summary: Lionel's many school-related adventures include a nervous
Back-to-School Night with his parents, the welcoming of a new classmate,
a sister who doesn't seem to recognize him, and an experiment with time.
ISBN 0-8037-2457-8
[1. Schools—Fiction.] I. Natti, Susanna, ill. II. Title. III. Series.
PZ7.K883Ls 2000 [Fic]—dc21 99-10695 CIP

Puffin Easy-to-Read ISBN 0-14-230137-X
Puffin® and Easy-to-Read® are registered trademarks of Penguin Putnam Inc.

Printed in Hong Kong

The full-color artwork was prepared using pencil, colored pencils, and watercolor washes.

Reading Level 2.2

CONTENTS

KEEPING SECRETS

It was Back-to-School Night

for grades one, two, and three.

Lionel and his parents arrived

a little late.

"Are you all right, Lionel?"

asked Mother.

"You took a long time

to tie your sneakers."

"I'm fine," said Lionel.

But he wasn't, not really.

His sister, Louise, had told him

what happened when parents

and teachers met.

"They trade secrets,"

she had explained.

"And then they know *everything*

about you."

Lionel had worried about this all day.

What would his parents

say to Mrs. Banks?

Would they tell her how he snuck

into their bed during thunderstorms?

And what would Mrs. Banks

tell his parents?

Would she describe how he talked

to the class fish?

Lionel frowned.

He wanted to keep

his secrets secret.

Mrs. Banks was waiting

outside the classroom.

"Hello, Lionel," she said.

"I'm glad you could come.

And these must be your parents."

Mrs. Banks shook their hands.

"Um, right this way,"

Lionel said quickly.

"I promise to show you *everything*."

Lionel explained to his parents
how his desk opened and shut.
"If you drop the top loudly,
you get in trouble," he told them.
Then he showed them a poem
he had written.
"You should read it all," he said.

Father picked up

several sheets of paper.

"This must have taken you

a long time," he said.

Lionel nodded.

When they were done,

Lionel put the poem back in the desk.

"Very interesting," said Father.

"Especially the part about the robot snowman," said Mother.

"Now, let's go talk with Mrs. Banks."

"Not yet," said Lionel.

"First we have to look at the picture I drew for the poem."

The picture was on the wall.

Lionel pointed out every single thing about it.

Then he showed them

the other pictures too.

"My favorite is Jeffrey's," he said.

"It's called *Aliens from the Wild*

Vegetable Planet."

"Terrific," said Mother.

"But we really should talk to—"

14

Lionel gasped.

"You haven't met the fish!"

He dragged them over to the fish tank.

He introduced each fish

and explained which ones

swam around a lot

and which ones blew big bubbles.

Suddenly, the bell rang.

"Uh-oh!" said Lionel. "We have to go."

"Already?" said Father.

"We didn't get to—"

"Sorry," said Lionel.

"Mrs. Banks will need to get home."

He led his parents out the door.

"Thanks, Mrs. Banks!" he shouted.

"We had a great time!"

Lionel smiled all the way

to the car.

He had kept his promise—

and his secrets too.

MOVING

Lionel sat down to breakfast.

First, he put a little cereal in his bowl.

Then he added a splash of milk.

"If you ate faster," said Louise,

"you wouldn't have to worry

about soggy cereal."

Lionel ignored her.

"We're getting a new boy

in our class today," he announced.

"His name is Ben."

"Where is he from?" asked Father.

Lionel wasn't sure.

He looked at the milk in the bowl.

It reminded him of snow.

"I hope it's someplace far away,"

he said.

"Like Alaska. Then he'll have

a lot of stories to tell

about wrestling with polar bears."

Louise shook her head.

"Where do you get these ideas?" she asked. "You don't even know if he likes polar bears."

Lionel put more milk in his bowl. The milk surrounded the cereal like an island.

"I guess Ben might be from
somewhere tropical," he said.
"Maybe a place where they surf to
school every morning."
"That's even more ridiculous,"
said Louise.
"Well," Mother added quickly,
"wherever he's from,
I'm sure he'd like a new friend."

The first thing

Mrs. Banks did that morning

was introduce Ben to the class.

Ben didn't say anything.

He just looked at the floor.

Lionel went over to him at recess.

"Hi!" he said. "I'm Lionel."

"Hello," said Ben, blushing.

"There's a lot of stuff

you should know about the school,"

Lionel went on.

"Like where the cold water fountain

is and which school lunches

you should *never* ever eat."

Ben nodded.

"So, tell me," said Lionel,

"what was it like

where you used to live?

Were there mountains of snow

or palm trees and coconuts?"

Ben shook his head.

"Nothing like that," he said.

"I just moved from across town."

"Oh." Lionel was disappointed.

He knew there were no polar

bears across town.

Or tidal waves either.

"But even in the same town," said Ben,

"I feel like I've moved to another planet.

I don't know any of the shortcuts

or which dogs are friendly."

"That does make it different,"

agreed Lionel.

Maybe how far you moved

wasn't important.

Maybe feeling at home

in *any* new place was hard.

"Don't worry, Ben," he said,

remembering what his mother

had told him.

"Here at school,

I will be your trusty guide.

But if you want to try any

mystery meat at lunch . . ."

"Yes?" asked Ben.

"You're on your own," said Lionel.

THE STRANGER

Lionel was walking down the hall.

Louise was coming the other way.

"Hi, Louise!" said Lionel.

Louise didn't seem to notice.

She kept on talking to her friends.

Lionel frowned.

Why didn't Louise recognize him?

He looked exactly like the Lionel

she had seen at breakfast.

This was very strange.

Later at recess,

Lionel chased a ball out of bounds.

It landed near Louise.

"Can you throw me the ball?"

he asked her.

But Louise didn't pick up the ball.

She just walked away.

Stranger and stranger, thought Lionel.

How could Louise not have heard him?

Something was wrong.

He discussed this with Jeffrey

and Max at lunch.

"Maybe she got hit on the head

and lost her memory,"

said Jeffrey.

Lionel didn't think so.

"Maybe she's fallen under someone else's control," said Max.

"Uh-oh!" said Jeffrey. "I just saw a movie about aliens taking over people's brains. Could that have happened to Louise?"

"It must have," said Lionel.

"We'll have to free her right away!"

"How?" Jeffrey asked.

Lionel had an idea.

"The alien signal must travel

through the air," he said.

"We have to interrupt it somehow."

"But what will stop such a thing?"

asked Max.

Lionel smiled.

"I think I know," he said.

When Louise got home that afternoon,

Lionel and Jeffrey jumped

out of the bushes beside her.

"What's going on?" she said.

"Now!" Lionel shouted,

shooting his water gun.

"The water will block the signal."

"*Aiieeeeeee!*" cried Louise,

throwing up her hands.

"What are you doing, Lionel!"

"It's working!" cried Jeffrey.

"She recognized you."

"Keep shooting!" said Lionel.

"We have to make sure."

In just a few seconds,

Louise was soaking wet.

"Lionel! Jeffrey!" she shouted.

"I can't believe you did this."

"You don't have to thank us,"

said Lionel.

"We know you would do

the same thing for us."

He explained to her about the aliens.

"And don't worry," he added.

"If it ever happens again . . ."

Lionel and Jeffrey pointed

their water guns at her.

"We'll be ready," they said together.

PASSING THE TIME

Lionel looked up from his desk

at the clock on the wall.

It was still ten whole minutes

till recess.

He squirmed in his seat.

Tick-tock. Tick-tock. Tick-tock.

The second hand on the clock

jerked from one second to the next.

These minutes were taking forever.

Finally, the bell rang.

"Hooray!" shouted Lionel.

He ran outside with everyone else.

Lionel played tag first.

He ran so fast

that nobody could catch him.

Then a bunch of kids

started playing kickball.

But when Lionel got his turn to kick,

the bell rang again.

Recess was over.

"Already?" said Lionel.

How could that be?

Recess always goes too fast,

he thought. And gym too.

But when he was sitting in class,

time went much slower.

And when I'm practicing

my handwriting, thought Lionel,

time goes slowest of all.

If only class time passed quickly

and recess passed slowly.

Could he make this happen?

Lionel thought about it for a while.

He remembered

that he moved fast at recess

and slower in the classroom.

Maybe if he made a switch—

and went slower at recess

and faster in the classroom—

he could change the way time worked.

The next morning at school,

Lionel tested out his idea.

He fed the class fish really fast.

Sprinkle, sprinkle, sprinkle.

Oops! thought Lionel,

looking at the food floating on the

water like a blanket.

A little too much.

He scooped the extra food back out,

splashing a lot of water on the floor.

"Uh-oh," he muttered.

As he was cleaning it up,

he glanced at the clock.

It was almost time for recess.

His plan was working!

When the recess bell rang,

Lionel went outside.

Suddenly, Jeffrey tagged him.

"You're it, Lionel!" he cried.

Then he dashed away.

Lionel just walked after him.

He didn't want to go faster

because that would make time

go faster too.

"Come on, Lionel," said Jeffrey.

"Don't be such a slowpoke."

Lionel hesitated,

but he stuck to his plan.

Pretty soon, though,

everyone was yelling at him.

"What's going on, slowpoke?"

"Is there cement in your sneakers?"

Lionel frowned.

Trying to make time pass quickly

in class had not really been fun.

And making time pass slowly

at recess was not fun at all.

Maybe, thought Lionel,

time knew what it was doing.

"Here I come!" he said.

Lionel ran like the wind.

With all the time he had wasted,

there wasn't a minute to spare.